Welcome to the Kingdom of Zork!

You are bored. There's nothing on TV except some stupid reruns. You wander into your local book store and pick up an interesting-looking book entitled *Zork: The Cavern of Doom*. As usual, you turn to the first page and begin reading.

The book is set in the magical land of Zork, where a new, incredibly rich underground realm has just been discovered. Dozens of adventurers have entered the Cavern of Doom, but none have returned. Only YOU can save them! There are bad-tempered warlocks, huge diamonds, dragons, and a giant empire to explore. It looks like this book is good!

Do you choose to save the kingdom? If so, purchase the book and turn to page 7.

Or do you choose to go home and watch reruns? Turn to the next page.

In front of the TV, your eyelids slowly close. A strange sound fills the room. Suddenly your eyes open; you realize that you have been snoring.

You can't get that Zork book out of your mind, but the book store is already closed.

Think again! Wouldn't it be wise to purchase the book now, and turn to page 7?

And watch for these WHAT-DO-I-DO-NOW BOOKS *available from Tor:*

ZORK: The Forces of Krill
ZORK: The Malifestro Quest

#3
THE CAVERN OF DOOM

S. ERIC MERETZKY

TOR

A TOM DOHERTY ASSOCIATES BOOK

Copyright©1983 by Infocom, Inc.

ZORK is a registered trademark of Infocom, Inc.

Interior illustrations by Dell Harris.

A TOR Book

Published by Tom Doherty Associates, 8-10 W. 36th St., New York, New York 10018

First printing, September 1983

ISBN: 0-812-57985-2

Printed in the United States of America

Distributed by Pinnacle Books, 1430 Broadway, New York, New York 10018

It is the first cool day after a week-long summer heat wave, so June and Bill are taking the opportunity to bicycle to Lookout Point in the hills outside of town. It is a favorite "secret spot" of theirs, and they come here often.

As the sun reaches its zenith they arrive at Lookout Point, a small plateau bordered on one side by rolling hills and on the other side by a steep cliff. They sit down under the familiar overhanging rock, which offers some protection from the bright midday sun. The edge of the cliff is just a few yards away. Neither of them speaks for a long while.

Finally, June breaks the silence. "You know what I've been thinking, Bill?"

Bill absent-mindedly tosses a pebble over the edge of the cliff. "I give up. What've you been thinking?"

"It's been two months since our last adventure . . ."

"That's funny—I've been thinking about the Land of Zork all day, also."

The Kingdom of Zork is a magical land far away, a land where Bill and June are known

Go to page 8.

as Bivotar and Juranda, a land ruled by their "uncle" Syovar. Twice before, Bill and June have ventured there, once battling the evil Krill, would-be conqueror of Zork, and once saving Syovar from the terrible wizard Malifestro.

Bill reaches into his pocket and removes the Ring of Zork, their gateway to the Land of

Go to page 9.

Zork. Placing the ring on one's finger some-how transports one to that amazing land. As Bill holds up the ring, sunlight glints off its golden surface.

Suddenly, a lizard scurries out from behind a clump of scrubgrass, startling Bill. He drops the Ring of Zork, which begins rolling along the rock toward the edge of the cliff. Bill and June both leap after it. Bill gasps as he slips on a patch of gravel at the cliff's edge. June grabs onto him, but they both lose their balance, and plunge over the precipice!

The ground rushes toward them. Sharp boulders beckon. Bill and June are too terri-fied even to scream.

Then, just before they hit the ground, the lighting changes. They land jarringly, but the fall is softened by a plush carpet. They look around in amazement, for they are in the throne room of the Castle of Zork! Moreover, they are dressed in adventurers' garb. Syovar stands with his back to them, apparently lost in thought. Through the wide doorways to the adjoining banquet hall, they can see a modest luncheon being served.

Go to page 11.

Syovar, hearing the commotion of their arrival, slowly turns. He notices them, and his face lights up. "Juranda and Bivotar! I was just thinking about you two. How wonderful that you decided to drop in."

"Well, it wasn't entirely intentional," begin Juranda. She explains what happened.

"Frobs above!" explains Syovar. "You two are pretty lucky. You must have been protected by the power of the ring. Or maybe it was the fact that I was thinking of you . . . Sometimes magic works in ways we don't understand."

As if to illustrate Syovar's last comment, the Ring of Zork suddenly appears in mid-air and falls to the floor. Syovar picks the ring up and puts it safely in his pocket.

"Well. There's a small banquet going on, and there'll be a play presented afterwards, I believe. Today is also the date of the jousting finals, on the meadow outside the castle. The competition begins in about an hour. Or, you can go to the annual crafts fair in the courtyard."

"Those all sound like fun," Juranda says.

Go to page 12.

"But what I would most like to do, if you're interested, is to go to my library and talk, and get to know each other better. I could tell you tales about the fall of the Great Underground Empire, and about the early campaigns against the evil Krill. I used to be considered a spellbinding storyteller."

"That sounds interesting," says Bivotar.

Go to the banquet and play?
Go to page 13.

Attend the jousting finals?
Go to page 15.

Visit the crafts fair?
Go to page 19.

Stay and listen to Syovar's stories?
Go to page 21.

"Let's go to the banquet," Bivotar decides. "I'm pretty hungry."

"Always found them to be noisy affairs," Syovar comments, "but if that's what you want . . ."

He leads them into the banquet hall, a huge room whose far wall is a tremendous mirror, and announces them. Most of the guests recognize Bivotar and Juranda from their previous visits to Zork, and they are greeted heartily.

Great platters of pheasant and wild boar are accompanied by an amazing variety of fresh breads, salads, and vegetables. Syovar performs several impressive magic tricks, including levitating the entire table. The jester, Perilon, performs some amusing skits. For dessert, the waiters bring out enormous trays heaped with exotic chocolates, and the finest fruits in season.

After the meal, the play begins, featuring a troupe of traveling actors. The play is fairly interesting, being about an aged wizard, exiled from his homeland, who has begun to lose his powers and amuses himself by harassing passing adventurers.

Go to page 14.

Finally, Bivotar and Juranda are escorted to the luxurious guest rooms of the castle.

The following morning, Juranda whispers to Bivotar, "You know, I've been feeling a little guilty. Syovar really seemed to want to spend some time alone with us."

"I've been thinking the same thing, Juran. Let's ask Syovar if we can do that today."

Go to page 21.

"I want to go to the banquet," states Bivo-tar.

"I'd like to see the crafts fair," Juranda argues.

They compromise on the jousting finals and tell Syovar of their decision.

"Always thought jousting was pretty bar-baric myself," Syovar comments. He accom-panies them out to the meadow beyond the castle moat. Large grandstands have been erected around the jousting area. Thousands of people from the surrounding towns fill the stands. Knights, their armor gleaming in the noontime sun, parade about on horseback. Brightly-colored banners flap in the breeze.

Syovar leads them to seats in the royal box as the tournament begins. The jousts are fierce and exciting, and the crowds cheer loudly. Elves wind through the stands, selling sweetmeats and rare fruits from far-off lands.

After the tournament is over, and Syovar has awarded ribbons to the winners, fires are lit and a gigantic barbecue begins. The smell of roasting steer fills the air. Wine and hearty ale flows freely. The celebration lasts long after nightfall.

Go to page 17.

The next morning, after a restful sleep, Syovar meets the two adventurers at breakfast. Bivotar glances at Juranda and then says to Syovar, "We were thinking last night, Juranda and I, that maybe, maybe we could hear your stories today?"

"Yes," Juranda adds, "we should've done it yesterday—I don't know why we decided to go to those jousts instead."

Go to page 21.

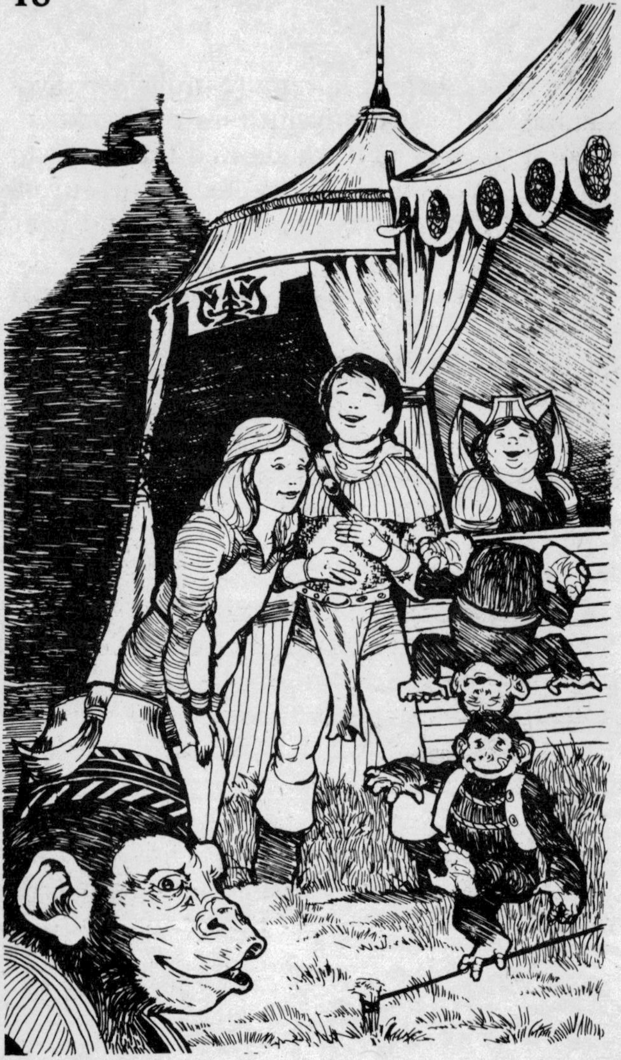

· "I'd really like to see the crafts fair," says Juranda.

"They usually bore me to tears," sighs Syovar, "but if you insist. . . ."

He takes them into the tremendous courtyard of the castle. Rows of booths line the walls, and the aisles are jammed with people. The odor of steaming figs wafts through the air. Monkeys, wearing brightly colored jackets, perform juggling acts and acrobatic tricks. A band of lute players adds to the festive atmosphere.

The booths display a stunning variety of items. Some dwarves from a kingdom far to the south display finely woven silk fabrics of every imaginable color. At the next booth are intricate straw baskets and chairs. The next table displays an amazing collection of tiny, beautifully hand-painted pottery bowls, designed to hold magic powders and ointments. Each booth is more intriguing than the last, and they wander down the aisles until twilight signals an end to the crafts fair.

Syovar leads them to the sumptuous guest rooms of the castle, where Bivotar and Juran-

Go to page 20.

da quickly fall into a deep sleep. The next morning, Bivotar pulls Juranda aside.

"I think that maybe we hurt Syovar's feelings yesterday by not letting him tell us his stories."

"Now that you mention it, Biv, he did look a little hurt when we told him we wanted to go to the crafts fair. But maybe he'll agree to do it today, instead."

"It's worth asking. I'd certainly like to hear him."

Go to page 21.

Syovar seems pleased by their decision, and leads them to his private study, a cozy room filled with books and ancient curios. A fire roars in the hearth.

As they munch on delicious cakes and sip a strange herbal tea, Syovar reminisces about his childhood days during the height of the Great Underground Empire. He recalls how he learned magic from an aged sorcerer named Hermacedus. Bivotar and Juranda are surprised to learn that Syovar was married once, during the last days before the fall of the Empire. His wife, Lorena, was killed by an enemy of Syovar, an evil warlock named Grawl. Grawl also cast a powerful spell on Syovar's only son, Logrumethar, and exiled him to a distant land. Syovar was never able to locate his son again, and has finally forced himself to admit that Logrumethar is dead.

As the fire grows dimmer, Syovar tells them of the rise and fall of the Great Underground Empire—a mighty kingdom carved right into the bedrock of the earth, a kingdom of wondrous sights, tremendous wealth, and powerful magic. But, because of the decadence of its

Go to page 22.

ruler, Lord Dimwit Flathead, the empire finally fell.

Following the fall, evil times came to the Land of Frobozz, as every warlock in the kingdom attempted to gain control. Finally, Syovar helped re-create the Knights of Zork, an ancient royal army, to help bring order to the land. With the defeat of Krill, the most powerful of the warlocks, peace returned.

Now the Great Underground Empire is rising once more. Each week, new areas of the old underground caverns are rediscovered, explored, and settled. Flood Control Dam Number Three is once again the famous tourist spot it was at the height of the empire, and the Mines of Zork are once again producing coal and diamonds. Syovar speaks softly of his dream of uniting all the neighboring lands into a peaceful, happy kingdom.

A troubled look comes over Syovar's face. "Recently," Syovar says, "explorers have discovered a new section of the Great Underground Empire, and adventurers and treasure hunters have flocked into the vast new area. None have returned.

Go to page 24.

"Several knights have gone in to search for the missing explorers, but they have not returned either. With utmost reluctance, I have been forced to seal up that section of the Underground Empire forever, to prevent more disappearances." Syovar pauses, and looks sadly toward Bivotar and Juranda. "Unfortunately, Max and Fred, the two elves who joined your quest to rescue me from the wizard Malifestro, are among the missing."

Syovar absent-mindedly strokes his beard. "I attempted to use my magical powers to explore this Cavern of Doom, but they were unable to penetrate it. It is as though the entire region were guarded by some powerful enchantment. All I could glean was a vague feeling that only someone completely innocent, only someone pure of heart, could enter that enchanted cavern and return."

Syovar pauses, lost in thought. The room has grown dark; the fire has turned into a bed of glowing embers. Syovar shakes himself out of his reverie. "Well, look how late it is! You two had best be off to your chambers." He summons a servant to escort them.

Go to page 25.

Later that night, Juranda quietly enters Bivotar's chamber. She wakes him gently. "Hey, Biv . . ."

"Hurglumph? Oh, it's you. What's up?"

"We've got to go to the Cavern of Doom."

"Sure," Bivotar says, rolling over. "First thing in the morning."

"I'm serious," insists Juranda.

Bivotar stares at her. "You must be wacko! You heard what Syovar said—no one has ever gone in there and returned!"

"But he also said that someone who was young and innocent could enter and return. We probably fit that bill as much as anyone around." Before Bivotar can object, Juranda hurriedly continues. "And we've got to find Max and Fred—they're our friends!"

Would you dare to enter the Cavern of Doom?
Go to page 26.

Otherwise, go to page 31.

Bivotar eventually agrees with Juranda, and the next morning at breakfast he broaches the subject to Syovar.

"Um, Syovar," Bivotar begins, "Juranda and I were talking last night and, uh, and we, uh. . . ."

"Yes?" asks Syovar, cracking open a dragon's egg.

"We want to go into the Cavern of Doom and rescue Max and Fred," Juranda blurts out.

Syovar looks flabbergasted. "Completely out of the question! It's far too dangerous!"

"But we can't just leave Max and Fred and all those others in there to die!" Bivotar protests.

"And you said yourself that someone pure of heart could enter the cavern and return," adds Juranda.

Syovar is silent for a time. The agony of indecision shows on his face. Finally, he nods slowly. "You two are both wise and brave. I cannot argue with your reasoning. However, remember that over fifty men, many of them also wise and brave, have gone into that

Go to page 27.

region and have never returned. Remember also that my powers cannot protect you there. Do you still wish to go?"

Bivotar and Juranda both nod solemnly.

"Very well. We will leave at once." Syovar reaches into his tunic and consults a parchment map. He mumbles a few spells under his breath, and motions with his arm. In a flash, they are all standing in a small underground hollow. Bivotar and Juranda are holding stout staffs. A tunnel slopes upward in one direction. In the other direction is a stone door. An inscription on the door reads:

As ruler of all the Kingdom of Zork
I hereby decree that this
Cavern of Doom
has been sealed off.
No man may remove the spell that protects this door.
No man may pass through into the cavern beyond.
Syovar

Syovar chants a long spell. At first, nothing happens. Then, slowly, the door swings open.

Go to page 29.

A cold wind swirls through the hollow where they stand.

"The cavern may now be entered," says Syovar. He hands them several bundles. "Here are several days' rations of food and water, and a lamp to light your way. And this is a powerful talisman." He hands Bivotar a beautiful amulet, carved from amber, suspended from an intricate golden chain. "It will glow in the presence of evil. The brighter the glow, the closer the evil."

Syovar places a hand on each of their heads and incants another spell. Then he says, "I have placed my strongest protection spell on you, but I cannot say whether it will work . . . in there. Remember that once you have entered, I will have to seal this entrance again. You will be totally alone."

"We understand," says Bivotar.

"Then farewell, and may the forces of good watch over you."

Bivotar and Juranda pass through the stone doorway. They glance back just in time to see the door close behind them.

Ahead, the tunnel forks. The left-hand pas-

Go to page 30.

sage seems to get a lot of use, because its dusty floor is covered with footprints. The other passage has a smoother, unmarked floor.

Take the left-hand passage? Go to page 33.

Take the smooth passage? Go to page 36.

Juranda finally gives in to Bivotar's objections and abandons her idea of venturing into the enchanted cavern.

The next morning, Syovar joins them for a modest breakfast, and then takes them to a nearby town to see a unicorn show. Finally, late in the day, Syovar admits that important affairs of state demand his attention. He bids

Go to page 32.

Juranda and Bivotar a fond farewell, and a
moment later they are back at Lookout Point.

THE END

*Your score is 0 out of a possible 10 points.
Well, you probably deserve another chance.
Turn to page 25 and try again.*

"Biv, let's take the passage with all the foot-prints. It's obviously the most often traveled path."

"Suits me," agrees Bivotar.

The passage descends sharply, and in many places there are steps carved into the stone floor to make travel easier. At the bottom of one such flight, they come across the skeleton of an unfortunate adventurer, his bones pick-ed clean by some carnivorous denizens of the Great Underground Empire. Lying next to the skeleton is an empty brown sack and a sturdy shovel.

Go to page 35.

"I'm going to hang onto this shovel," says Juranda.

"Might be useful," agrees Bivotar.

Further along, the passage ends at a large cavern. A stream runs through the center of the cavern. At the water's edge stands a large stone hut.

"It looks deserted," says Bivotar, peering in a window of the hut.

"Good place to eat lunch, I'd say."

Enter the stone hut?
 Go to page 38.

Avoid the stone hut?
 Go to page 41.

After a brief argument, Bivotar and Juranda agree to take the smoother passage.

The tunnel, which is fairly tight to begin with, grows increasingly smaller as they move further along. In addition, interesting rows of stalagmites and stalactites begin appearing. Unlike normal rocky formations in caverns, these appear only at the left and

Go to page 37.

right sides of the tunnel. Also, they are strange in both texture and color, smooth and pearly white. Finally, unlike normal stalactites and stalagmites, they are slightly curved.

Soon the tunnel has grown so tiny that Bivotar and Juranda are forced to drop to their hands and knees and crawl forward.

"Doesn't the ground feel unusually soft?" asks Bivotar.

"Yes. And sort of slimy, too," Juranda adds.

"Maybe we ought to go back to the fork and try that other passage."

Would you try the other tunnel?
Go to page 33.

Or, do you think it would be a better idea to continue along this tunnel?
Go to page 43.

Bivotar and Juranda enter the stone hut. The entire first floor seems to be one large room, with a small wooden table and some chairs. They sit at the table and eat a hurried lunch from the provisions that Syovar gave them.

"Let's have a look around," suggests Bivotar.

A brief inspection of the room reveals nothing of interest. However, a stone staircase spirals downward, indicating a cellar below. Warily, they descend the stairs, and find themselves in a musty chamber filled with cobwebs. Wooden tables line the room, covered with many curious items: scrolls of parchment, a stuffed owl, a rack of wands, and bottles of liquid and powder.

Suddenly, Juranda notices the talisman that Syovar gave them. "Biv, look at the amulet. It's beginning to glow. Syovar told us that meant there was evil nearby."

Bivotar examines the talisman. "It's only glowing very faintly. Syovar also said that if evil was close by, it would glow very brightly."

Go to page 40.

"Look at this," Juranda calls, pointing to a sign on the wall.

> This workroom and its contents
> are the property of Grawl.
> Anyone who disturbs my possessions
> shall be punished.

"Didn't Syovar mention that Grawl was a powerful and evil warlock?" asks Juranda.

"Yeah, I think so. Hey, look at this!" Bivotar picks up one of the parchment scrolls. "It's a spell for speaking with beasts in their own tongue. That sounds as if it might be fun." He puts the scroll in his pack.

"Biv!" Juranda cries. "The amulet is glowing brighter! We'd better get out of here."

"But there are still a lot of interesting things here," Bivotar protests.

Would you leave now, as Juranda suggests?
Go to page 41.

Would you stay and continue examining the warlock's curios? *Go to page 45.*

Leaving the hut behind them, Bivotar and Juranda wade the shallow stream and cross the cavern. At the far end of the cavern, a dark opening leads to another passage.

They enter this new tunnel. The ground here is made of soft sand, slowing their progress.

After walking for a while, they come to a point where the passage widens to form a small round room. In the center of the room, painted right onto the sandy floor, is a red "X".

" 'X' marks the spot," says Bivotar with a grin.

Go to page 42.

"What do you mean?"

"Try digging there with the shovel."

"Come on, Biv. What would that accomplish?"

"Who knows? It won't hurt to try."

"It'll just be a waste of time."

Try digging where the "X" is?
Go to page 48.

Forget the "X" and continue down the passage?
Go to page 50.

Juranda and Bivotar continue to crawl along the small tunnel with the slimy floor and the strange rock formations. The air is warm and moist.

Suddenly the floor begins vibrating strangely, and the walls of the tunnel begin contracting around them.

"What's going on?" shouts Juranda, confused.

Go to page 44.

"I don't know, but let's get out of here," yells Bivotar, crawling back toward the fork. "The amulet has started to glow!"

"Omigosh! Biv, we're not in a tunnel! And those aren't stalactites—they're teeth!"

"Burp!" says the cave behemoth, a short time later.

THE END

Your score is 1 out of a possible 10 points. Well, you probably deserve another chance. Turn to page 37 and try again.

Juranda paces nervously as Bivotar continues to search through Grawl's curios and potions.

"Look at this, Juran!" Bivotar takes a pinch of black powder from a jar and tosses it toward the ground. A giant puff of blue smoke appears. The smoke clears, revealing a tiny newt, which scurries off into the shadows. "Not bad, huh?"

Suddenly, they hear from upstairs the sound of the hut's door closing. The amulet glows strongly. There is a loud cry of anger, and then a small and shriveled man comes flying down the staircase. "Thieves! Vandals!" he cries, in a voice that is considerably more menacing than his appearance. He extends a crooked hand toward Juranda and Bivotar. A

Go to page 47.

bolt of light leaps toward them, and suddenly the newt has company in the shadows.

THE END

Your score is 2 out of a possible 10 points. Well, you probably deserve another chance. Turn to page 40 and try again.

Juranda shrugs and hands the shovel to Bivotar. He immediately begins digging into the sand at the center of the "X."

"You're just wasting time," Juranda complains.

Bivotar digs the hole deeper. The sand keeps sliding back into the hole, making his work difficult. Juranda whistles a tune.

"Had enough yet?" Juranda asks, several minutes later.

Go to page 49.

"Yeah, I guess so," says Bivotar, smiling. "I don't think I'll find anything besides this." He holds up a giant ruby, still covered with wet sand.

"Gosh! You were right, Biv. Wow!"

"Okay." Bivotar cleans the sand off the ruby and stows it in his pack. "Let's get going."

"Wait!" says Juranda. "Let's keep digging! There might be more rubies or there might . . ." She trails off, looking extremely embarrassed at her greedy outburst. "Yup, let's get going."

Go to page 50.

They proceed along the passageway. Here and there, smaller passages branch off to the side. The walls of the passage are black and lumpy. At various points, wooden beams have been erected to support the ceiling.

The passageway widens, and they notice a pair of parallel metal strips, like railroad tracks, running along the center of the passage.

"Juran, you know what I think this is? A coal mine!"

Juranda snaps her fingers. "You're right! And by the looks of it, it hasn't been used in a long time."

They follow the tunnel around a corner, and come upon a car of some kind, its four wheels mounted on the track. Most of the car is a large bin, filled with coal.

Next to the car is a strange sight—a wide doorway to a brightly lit room beyond. The room seems out of place here in the coal mine, especially its white polished granite walls.

Sitting in the center of the strange side room is an even stranger-looking machine.

"Let's take a closer look at that peculiar

Go to page 52.

machine," says Juranda.

"Oh, let's keep going," says Bivotar.

Approach the strange machine?
  Go to page 53.

Keep going?
  Go to page 57.

They enter the brightly lit room with the granite walls and approach the strange machine. It is shaped vaguely like a washing machine, with white enamel sides and a large lid on top. The controls consist of one solitary button. A label on the front of the machine, faded but still legible, says

Frobozz Magic Compressor

Some fine print beneath the name is too faded to read.

"Try pressing the button," suggests Juranda.

Bivotar presses the button. The machine comes to life with a dazzling display of colored lights and bizarre noises. After a few moments, the display ends.

"Interesting, but not very productive," Bivotar comments.

Juranda opens the lid and looks inside the machine. "It's empty," she says. "Let's try putting something inside, and then turning it on again."

"Like what?" asks Bivotar, looking through his possessions.

"How about some coal from out there in

Go to page 54.

that car?" Juranda leaves for a moment and returns with an armload of coal. She dumps the coal into the machine and closes the lid.

"Here goes," Bivotar says as he pushes the button. The machine reacts as it did before. When the display of lights and noise has subsided, Juranda opens the lid.

"Look!" she gasps, withdrawing a huge diamond.

"Wow!"

"But of course! It's a compressor. Remember? Diamonds are just coal that has undergone tremendous pressure!" She puts the diamond in her pack.

"Well, let's get going."

"But, wait a minute," says Bivotar. "There's a lot of coal out there in that bin. We could make a whole bunch of these diamonds!"

"That isn't what we came here for," protests Juranda.

Stay and produce some more diamonds?
  Go to page 56.

Continue into the depths of the Underground Empire?
  Go to page 57.

"Well, okay," says Juranda. "I guess it wouldn't hurt to make a few more diamonds . . ."

Bivotar dashes out to the car and returns with an armful of coal. While Juranda operates the compressor, Bivotar goes to get another armful. Soon they have produced a small pile of diamonds.

Unfortunately, the fine print on the label, which was too faded for Juranda or Bivotar to read, was a warning message. The warning explained that using a Frobozz Magic Compressor more than three times in one day can cause the machine's delicate magic circuits to overload. Sure enough, in the middle of producing a diamond, the compressor explodes. The resulting pyrotechnic display removes Bivotar, Juranda, and a good chunk of the coal mine.

THE END

Your score is 3 out of a possible 10 points. Well, you probably deserve another chance. *Turn to page 54 and try again.*

Bivotar and Juranda continue to traverse the coal mine. After a while, the tracks disappear, and the walls become gray and rocky again.

The air grows moist, and at various points trickles of water run down the walls of the tunnel. Dark green mosses grow abundantly where these trickles appear. Just beyond a particularly thick growth of mosses, they come to a small tunnel leading off from the main one.

Go to page 59.

Bivotar shines the lantern into the small side tunnel. It is very short, forming a dead end forty or fifty feet away. Sitting on the ground, just before the end wall, is a wooden trunk, bulging with jewels!

On the floor of the side passage, between the trunk and the two adventurers, is a carpet of green plants. They sway slowly from side to side, which is rather odd since there is almost no breeze in the tunnel.

"Juran! Look at that trunk of jewels! Let's take a closer look."

"Wait," cautions Juranda. "Those plant things might not be as harmless as they look."

Go down the side tunnel to the trunk of jewels?
Go to page 60.

Continue along the main passage?
Go to page 62.

Bivotar laughs at Juranda. "What, are you afraid of a few little plants? You can wait here, then." He starts toward the trunk of jewels.

"Wait, I'll come too." She follows after him, not noticing that the amulet has begun to glow.

They begin wading through the carpet of plants, which continues to ripple despite the lack of air currents. Just when they reach the

Go to page 61.

center of the patch of plants, it erupts about them!

The plants turn out to be a colony of whip-weeds, small green animals with poisonous stingers which imitate plants to lure their un-suspecting victims closer. Pulling their "roots" from the ground, they swarm all over Bivotar and Juranda, wrapping their poison-filled stingers around the unfortunate adven-turers.

THE END

Your score is 3 out of a possible 10 points. Well, you probably deserve another chance. Turn to page 59 and try again.

"Well, yeah, okay," says Bivotar, looking longingly back at the trunk filled with emeralds and sapphires. "Who needs jewels and stuff anyway, right?"

They follow the main passage for a long time. At one point, they surprise a family of bats, which go flying down the tunnel and disappear. Other than that, their travel is without incident, and they begin to get very bored and tired. Finally, they see a junction of some kind ahead. They reach the interesting corridor, which is much smaller and narrower.

To the left, the small corridor ends almost immediately. Just before this dead end, a dark hole leads downward. A rope, tied to a nearby

Go to page 63.

rock, dangles down into the hole. Sinister gurgling noises can be heard from below.

To the right, the passage continues beyond the range of the lantern. However, the ground in that direction is strewn with bones.

Straight ahead is a metal gate, blocking off the main passage. Just behind the gate, sound asleep, is a hairy gnome. He is very fat, and the remains of a half-eaten meal lie strewn about him.

Suddenly, a massive stone door descends from the ceiling just behind them and crashes shut. Echoes from the crash reverberate throughout down the tunnels. The gnome wakens instantly, and jumps to his feet.

"Ahah! Travelers!" begins the gnome, with

Go to page 64.

an artificial smile. "There hasn't been much traffic recently. I suppose you'll be wanting to come through the gate here?"

"Why yes, we would," answers Bivotar.

"I hope you're prepared to pay the toll," says the gnome, still smiling.

"What sort of toll?" asks Juranda, suspiciously.

Go to page 65.

"Oh, nothing much. A bauble. Actually, at this particular point in time, I'm feeling particularly fond of rubies."

Did you find the ruby?
If so, to go page 66.

If not, you will have to try one of the two side passages.

If you choose the dark hole, go to page 68.

If you choose the tunnel strewn with bones, go to page 71.

"Okay," grumbles Bivotar, removing the giant ruby from his pack. "Take this ruby."

The gnome takes the ruby. He reaches into his vest and withdraws a jeweler's loupe. He carefully examines the ruby through the magnifier.

"It is a fine gem, but somewhat small," the gnome grumbles. "I'm afraid it is too puny to suffice for the toll. However, perhaps if you had another jewel. . . ."

"What if we refuse to pay your toll?" asks Juranda. "How about if we just climb over your dumb gate and keep going?"

"That would be most annoying," responds the gnome, smiling even more broadly. "In that case, I would be forced to summon my colleague, Tholl. He's a rather large troll. Tholl the Toll Troll, they call him. And while he's not very bright, he is quite vicious. Now, about that second jewel. . . ."

Did you create the diamond?
  If so, go to page 74.

If not, you will have to choose between the two side passages.
  Dark hole? Go to page 68.
  Bone-littered tunnel? Go to page 71.

"We won't be able to pay the toll, Biv."

"Yeah, well, nuts to that fat old gnome, anyway. Let's go this way instead." He heads off toward the dark hole.

Juranda looks down into the hole. "It's pretty dark down there, and if we have to climb down on this rope we won't be able to carry anything."

"I don't care, as long as I never see that grinning gnome again." Bivotar drops the lantern and his pack and begins climbing down the rope. Juranda puts her own possessions down, and follows.

The rope ends a few feet above the ground. The only thing they can see is a faint circle of light above them—the hole they just climbed down—and the faintly glowing amulet. From the darkness around them come loud, gurgling sounds.

Unfortunately, Bivotar and Juranda have dropped right into a well-populated grue lair. Grues are vicious carnivorous beasts that occupy every dark corner of the Great Underground Empire. Their favorite diet is adventurers, and their only fear is that of light.

Go to page 70.

Their fangs are long, sharp, and numerous, which they waste no time in demonstrating to our hapless heroes.

THE END

Your score is 4 out of a possible 10 points. Well, you probably deserve another chance. Turn to page 42 and try again.

"We're getting nowhere with this guy," says Bivotar, clenching his fists.

"Forget about that dumb gnome and his dumb toll gate. Let's go this way." Juranda leads Bivotar into the tunnel littered with bones.

"I don't like the look of this tunnel," comments Bivotar.

"You can't be scared of a few old bones," Juranda answers.

After walking for two minutes, they come to an ornate wooden door. There is a sign on the door engraved in a flowery script:

May Eternal Peace Be Yours

"Sounds intriguing, Juran. Let's go in."

They open the door and enter a dimly lit room. The floor is covered with a plush carpet, and the walls seem to be covered with velvet.

"Welcome to the Frobozz Magic Crematorium," says the welcoming robot, shutting and locking the door behind him. The robot appears to be rusty and in need of repair. He gives off occasional sparks and puffs of smoke.

Go to page 72.

"Are these stiffs ready yet, Leo?" says a second robot, floating toward them. The second robot also seems to be old and damaged.

"Stiffs? What are you talking about?" Bivotar demands.

"Hey, Rocky, I don't remember corpses ever talking before," remarks the robot called Leo.

"Ah, who can remember," Rocky replies. "It's been a hundred and forty-two years since

Go to page 73.

the last stiff. I'll be lucky if I remember how to use the equipment."

"Hey! Now wait a minute. . . ." Juranda is cut short as the robots grab her and Bivotar and drag them into the Frobozz Magic Incinerator. Leo shuts the door as Rocky begins to press the buttons, humming with contentment.

A bit later, Leo opens the door and floats into the chamber. Nothing remains except a pile of bones. "Hey, Rocky! Your turn to take out the bones!"

THE END

Your score is 4 out of a possible 10 points. Well, you probably deserve another chance. *Turn to page 42 and try again.*

"Here," says Juranda, reaching into her pack. "Take this diamond, only let us by!"

"Patience, patience," scolds the gnome. He examines the diamond through his loupe. "It is, once again, a fine gem. However, it is also rather puny."

"Are you going to let us by or not?" shouts Bivotar, losing his temper.

"Well, I suppose I will accept these baubles this time. However, don't expect me to accept such a paltry toll the next time you pass this way." Moving slowly, the gnome unlocks the gate and swings it open. Bivotar and Juranda pass through, glaring at the greedy gnome, and continue down the passage.

A short time later, the passage widens into a large cavern. The air in the cavern is quite chilly.

"Look!" gasps Bivotar, pointing. One side of the cavern is a giant wall of ice, the tip of some subterranean glacier. Its surface is smooth and shiny, reflecting their lantern light like an enormous mirror.

"It's beautiful," Juranda whispers.

After admiring the mirror of ice for a few

Go to page 76.

more moments, they cross the cavern and continue down the passage. The air grows warmer again, and the walls of the passage here seem scarred and blackened as if by some tremendous heat.

The passage turns a corner and suddenly opens into another wide cavern. The floor of the cavern is strewn with rocks and boulders. Sitting in the center of the cavern is a mighty dragon, smoke curling from his nostrils!

Did you get the spell for talking to beasts in their own tongue?

If so go to page 77.

If not, go to page 80.

As they enter the dragon's room, the dragon gives a deep-throated roar, and moves to block the tunnel on the far side of the cavern.

"That dragon looks pretty mean," says Juranda.

"Juran, I have an idea. Let's try casting that spell for talking to animals. Maybe we can convince him that we're friendly."

"Good idea!" Juranda unrolls the spell scroll, looks at the dragon, and chants, "Utteryak parlo babalon nitfol verbalate."

Gradually, the dragon's roar seems to coalesce into understandable language. "Begone, little creatures," the rumble seems to be saying. "You cannot pass by Leblong the Dragon."

"We mean you no harm, Leblong," Bivotar shouts. "We only wish to continue on our journey."

The dragon gives a bellowing laugh, which shakes the cavern walls and covers Bivotar and Juranda with a cloud of ash and smoke. "Not a chance, little one. I guard this cavern because of an agreement with the great warlock Grawl. He agreed to dispose of my

Go to page 79.

treacherous twin brother Berlong. In exchange, I promised to guard this tunnel from trespassers for the next thousand years."

"And is there no way that you would break this oath?" asks Juranda.

"Only if I saw my despicable twinling Berlong again. Then I would know that Grawl had failed to honor his part of the bargain, and I would no longer feel duty-bound to follow my promise."

Try to kill the dragon?
  Go to page 82. (You might want to try to think of a way to kill the dragon before continuing.)

Try to trick the dragon?
  Go to page 84. (You might want to try to think of a way to trick the dragon before continuing.)

Try to sneak past the dragon?
  Go to page 88. (You might want to try to think of a way to sneak past the dragon before reading on.)

As Bivotar and Juranda enter the dragon's lair, the dragon gives a deep growl and a plume of hot steam pours from its nostrils. It waves its head toward them, growls again, and then lets loose a mighty roar. A hot cloud of smoke washes across the two adventurers.

"He doesn't seem too friendly," comments Bivotar.

"It's almost as though he was trying to tell us something," Juranda notes.

"Unfortunately, I don't know dragonese, or whatever it is that dragons speak."

Go to page 81.

"Well, let's not mess with it. Let's just go around the edge of this cavern and continue on down the passage."

"Fine by me," agrees Bivotar.

As they attempt to pass by the dragon, it bellows a deep-throated roar, rears its head back, and spews a gigantic plume of flame straight at Bivotar and Juranda. They are instantly fried to a crisp.

THE END

Your score is 5 out of a possible 10 points. Well, you probably deserve another chance. Turn to page 40 and try again.

"He's not going to let us through," whispers Bivotar.

"I know," answers Juranda. "We'll have to kill him."

"How?"

"Look at all these rocks on the ground," says Juranda pointing. "We'll each take a few, climb up on those boulders over there, and pummel him with the rocks. We'll aim for the head."

Bivotar looks skeptical, but joins Juranda in gathering up several large stones. When they are in position, Juranda gives the signal, and they hurl the rocks toward Leblong's head.

Unfortunately, dragon hide is very tough, and the rocks bounce harmlessly off. However, they do seem to enrage Leblong, who roars indignantly, draws back, and expels a terrific blast of fire toward them. Bivotar and Juranda are reduced to ashes.

THE END

Your score is 6 out of a possible 10 points. Well, you probably deserve another chance. Turn to page 79 and try again.

"We'll never get past that dragon," says Bivotar. "We'd better turn back."

"Not so fast, Biv. I've got an idea." Juranda calls out to the dragon: "Leblong, did you say that the warlock Grawl vowed to kill your twin brother Berlong?"

"That is true," the dragon rumbles.

"That's funny, because we just saw Berlong a little way back."

Leblong eyes Juranda warily. "How do you know it was Berlong?"

"He told us," answers Bivotar, jumping in. "Besides, he looked exactly like you."

"He said that if we should happen to run into you, we should tell you that he's waiting for you," adds Juranda.

The dragon thinks for a moment. "I don't believe you," he announces finally.

"Then come with us, and we'll lead you to him!"

Leblong thinks for a long time again. "I will come," he growls, "but I won't let either of you out of my sight for a moment, and if either of you should attempt to slip past me, I will burn you in an instant."

Go to page 85.

"Good enough," answers Juranda bravely. "Follow."

Juranda and Bivotar precede Leblong, leading the dragon back along the passage. Presently, they arrive back at the cool cavern with the mirror of ice.

"There," yells Juranda, pointing at the glacier. "There is Berlong!"

Leblong looks at the ice and sure enough—he sees what appears to be his treacherous twin brother. While dragons are not stupid, they are often naive, and this dragon has spent most of his life sitting in one room. He has never seen ice, or a mirror, and so who can blame him when he mistakes his own reflection for his hated twin brother?

Leblong rears back on his powerful hind legs and bellows a fiery challenge. The reflection responds in kind! The dragon then directs a gout of fire right at his foe, followed by another, and another. The flame washes across the ice, which begins to melt. Leblong sees his enemy unharmed, and redoubles his efforts. Barrages of fire strike the ice. Torrents of water begin pouring off the glacier,

Go to page 87.

swirling about the room.

Juranda and Bivotar are swept off their feet by a wave of water, and are washed down a tunnel away from the glacier cavern. Waves of icy water splash all about them. Finally, the waters recede, and they find themselves in the middle of the room where they first met the dragon. Leblong is nowhere in sight.

"Wow! Close call, that time," says Juranda, wringing water from her clothes.

"Nice thinking there, Juran."

"Well, it's safe to continue now. Let's get going before Leblong comes back."

Bivotar begins picking up their possessions. As he lifts the lamp, he moans, "Oh, no! Just what we need. The lamp looks like it's going out!"

Juranda examines it. "It must have gotten damaged by the water." Even as she speaks, the light from the lamp grows dimmer.

Did you get the scroll with the light spell from the rockworm tribe?

If so, go to page 91.

If not, go to page 94.

"Doesn't look like that dragon will let us pass, Biv."

"Yeah, but I bet we can sneak by him. He doesn't seem that bright."

"Do you have a plan?"

"Yup. First we convince the dragon that we've left. Then we'll sneak around the edge

Go to page 89.

of the cavern, behind all those boulders."

"Sounds good to me," agrees Juranda.

Bivotar raises his voice. "Well, we'd better be going. Farewell, Leblong!"

"Farewell, flameless ones," Leblong rumbles.

Bivotar leads Juranda toward the mouth of the tunnel they recently left. Just before they reach it, they duck behind one of the larger boulders.

"Okay," Bivotar whispers. "I think we fooled him. Follow me."

They begin winding around the perimeter of the cavern, darting from behind one boulder to the next.

"Almost there," says Bivotar in a hushed voice. "Just one more gap to cross."

They scurry toward the cover of the final boulder. The mouth of the other passage looms ahead. Just before they reach the last boulder, Bivotar trips on a small rock and goes sprawling. Juranda rushes to help him to his feet. The dragon, hearing the noise, turns toward them.

"No one sneaks past Leblong!" roars the

Go to page 90.

dragon. He raises up to his full height (about thirty feet), stares down at them, and then burns them to cinders with a blast of flaming breath.

THE END

Your score is 6 out of a possible 10 points. Well, you probably deserve another chance. Turn to page 79 and try again.

A bolt of lightning crashes across the sky, and explodes to the ground at your feet. There is a puff of smoke, and the Prince of Kaldorn appears before you. Startled, you drop the book you are reading.

The Prince bends down and picks it up. He reads the cover of the book. "Hmmm . . . let's see. *The Cavern of Doom*." He produces a notebook and begins making an entry.

Until recently, the Prince of Kaldorn was living in exile and working as a shoe peddler. Recently, though, he has been appointed As-

Go to page 93.

sistant Third Class in the Anti-Cheating Bureau of Zorkbooks, Inc., whose job it is to prevent exactly the sort of brazen fraudulence you have just displayed.

The Prince finishes his notation. "I have taken down the name and serial number of this book," the Prince explains. "Since there are no light spells or rockworm tribes in this book, it is clear that you were cheating. If you repeat this offense, you will be turned into a newt." He wags his finger at you, and then vanishes.

THE END

Your score is so low that mathematicians have not yet invented a number to describe it.

Normally, I'd recommend giving you another chance, but not in this case, cheater!

The light from the lamp sputters and grows even dimmer. The gloom of the cavern closes in about them.

"This is terrible," moans Juranda. "Without the lamp we can't go on. We must turn back."

"We can't turn back now, Juran. I have a feeling we're getting really close to the end of our journey."

Go to page 95.

"But you know how dangerous the underground is with no light! We can always try again later."

"Well, if the light goes out, we'll never make it back anyway," Bivotar argues. "We might as well continue."

Continue without light?
  Go to page 96.

Turn back while you still have the chance?
  Go to page 100.

"Okay, you're right," concedes Juranda. "Let's continue. But we'd better hurry."

They enter the tunnel that was previously guarded by Leblong the dragon. It is straight and level, and they travel quickly. The lantern grows even dimmer. Finally, after about five minutes, the lamp goes out completely, leaving Bivotar and Juranda surrounded by darkness. They hear a gurgling noise close by, accompanied by what could be the sound of gnashing teeth.

At that moment, Juranda notices a spot of light in the distance ahead of them. She grabs Bivotar and points it out. "Come on," she cries, "let's make a run for it!"

From behind them comes a cry of anger, as the lurking creature senses its prey escaping. There are sounds of pursuit. Bivotar and Juranda run even faster toward the growing circle of light. Juranda stumbles over something in the darkness and drops her pack, but regains her balance. With a final burst of speed, they fly out of the dark tunnel and into a lighted area. From behind them comes a cry of pain and fear, and they turn just in time to

Go to page 98.

see a creature with enormous fangs turn and dash back into the darkness.

"Whew," exclaims Bivotar, his chest heaving. "Another close call."

"I dropped all the food while running," says Juranda. "I'm sorry."

"And I dropped the lamp, although I guess it's not much good any more anyway. But at least you managed to hang onto the talisman." Juranda glances down at the magic amulet, which is dark.

They turn to survey their new locale, and are greeted by an amazing sight: an enormous cavern, easily a mile across, filled with rock formations of every imaginable shape. The ceiling, far above, is covered with layer upon layer of phosphorescent mosses, glowing with every color of the rainbow. The floor of the cavern is covered with literally hundreds of stone statues, life-sized figures of knights, explorers, adventurers, and elves. The closest of these statues is only a few feet away.

"These statues are amazing, Biv. They're so life-like."

Bivotar examines one of the statues more

Go to page 99.

closely. "Juran . . . these aren't statues." His voice fills with fear. "They're people . . . people turned to stone!"

Suddenly a voice calls out to them. It is a hoarse croak, inhuman and horrible to hear. "Go away! Leave Grum alone. Please come in not here. Sorry will you be, yes." The owner of the voice is hidden from view among the statues. There is another exit just to their left.

Heed the words of the unseen creature and go away? Go to page 102.

Ignore the warning and enter this cavern?
Go to page 104.

"Okay, we'll do it your way," says Bivotar. They turn back in the direction of the glacier room. The light continues to dim. When they reach the glacier cavern, they find Leblong asleep, worn out from his amazing battle. He snores loudly, and with every snort a little puff of flame emerges from his nostrils, lighting up the whole cavern. There is no sign at all of the ice; it has melted completely away.

"Hurry up," says Juranda, tugging at Bivotar's arm. They continue toward the gnome's toll gate. A few hundred yards beyond the glacier room, the lantern gives a final flicker and dies. Bivotar and Juranda are left in pitch blackness.

Several gurgling noises immediately come from the darkness around them. The sounds can only mean one thing—a pack of grues, the fearsome creatures that inhabit every dark corner of the Great Underground Empire. Their insatiable hunger is tempered only by their fear of light. It is only the slightest consolation to Bivotar and Juranda that they

Go to page 101.

never get to see the enormous slavering fangs
which tear them apart.

THE END

*Your score is 7 out of a possible 10 points.
Well, you probably deserve another chance.
Turn to page 95 and try again.*

Bivotar and Juranda enter the new passage. After a short distance, it ends at a narrow stairway leading upward, lined with flickering torches. They climb the stairs, which are hundreds of steps tall. Finally the stairs end, and they enter a small torchlit room filled with countless treasures, many dusty sacks, and a scattering of bones. It is apparently the secret hideout of an underground robber.

There is a scream of anguish in the air. Armed with a silver stiletto, glinting in the torchlight, a lean man suddenly appears in the doorway and eyes them warily.

The magic amulet glows brightly.

He notices the amulet and, speaking with a coarse voice in some ancient and forgotten language, makes it clear that he wants to add the amulet to his collection of treasures. When Bivotar and Juranda do not respond, he lashes out with his stiletto. Being unarmed, Bivotar and Juranda find the battle a trifle one-sided.

THE END

Your score is 8 out of a possible 10 points. Well, you probably deserve another chance. Turn to page 99 and try again.

"We'd better listen to him, Juran."

"I'm not so sure," says Juranda. "These statues, all these people—these must be the explorers who have entered the Cavern of Doom but never returned! They're all right here!"

"Then let's get out of here before we turn to stone, also!"

"Biv, the amulet isn't glowing. So there's no evil here."

Bivotar thinks for a minute, then nods. "Okay. Let's go meet our unseen companion."

They take a few more steps into the cavern,

Go to page 105.

toward the hidden creature. They are now surrounded on all sides by the stone figures. Suddenly, the voice cries out again.

"Please, come not any closer! You, too, turned into stone will be!"

They pause, and catch a glimpse of a figure darting behind a group of statues, as though hiding. Bivotar calls out, "Who are you?"

"Called Grum am I. Live here I do."

"Grum, how did all these people turn to stone?" Juranda asks.

"The work of a terrible warlock it is. His name cannot I even remember. A powerful enchantment he cast on Grum. He make Grum hideous and horrible and ugly. Now, anyone who looks at Grum, turned to stone are they."

"Why did the warlock do this to you?" inquires Bivotar.

"Do not I even know. For long time, Grum here in this room has lived. No friends have I, no one can I ever talk to."

"Oh, Biv! He must be so lonely." Juranda calls to Grum, "Why do you stay here? Is it part of the spell?"

"No, not part of spell. I stay so that no one

Go to page 106.

can see Grum's ugliness. Turn others to stone I did not want to do. When those people started coming here, so happy was I. Coming to see Grum they were, I thought. But as soon as they saw me, statues did they become. Now, quickly go you should, or see me you may and turn to statues like others." Despite the unnatural timbre of the voice, it is filled with sadness and compassion.

"How can we help him, Biv? We've got to find a way to break the enchantment."

A rasping sound can be heard from Grum's direction.

"He's . . . he's crying," says Juranda, sniffling a bit herself.

"I don't care if he's the ugliest thing in the universe," Bivotar announces. "He's lonely, and he's in pain. I'm going to go meet him."

"Biv!" cries Juranda, but he is already running toward Grum. Grum sees him approaching, and tries to run away but falls to the ground. "No, come not closer," he wails, trying to hide his face.

Bivotar passes the last few statues and arrives at Grum's side. He is indeed ugly beyond

Go to page 107.

belief, scaly and deformed. But Bivotar ignores the ugliness, looking only at Grum's wide, compassionate eyes. Slowly, Grum lowers his arms, trembling with disbelief.

"You . . . you do not turn to statue. . . ."

Juranda arrives and kneels next to Bivotar.

"You're not so horrible," Juranda tells Grum.

"She's right, Grum. There are other kinds of beauty besides outward appearance. There's beauty of the soul. And by trying to warn us not to come here, and by living alone here for so long rather than risk harming others, you have demonstrated your inner beauty."

Tears stream down Grum's face. "Never imagined did I that anyone would ever call me beautiful."

"Grum, return with us to the world above," suggests Juranda.

"No!" Grum cries. "Too dangerous that would be!"

"But we have shown you that everyone who sees you doesn't turn to stone," argues Juranda.

Go to page 109.

"And we know a very good wizard who might be able to break your enchantment," adds Bivotar.

"Well, perhaps," Grum agrees, "but if just one more person becomes a statue, right back here will Grum go."

"Fair enough," Bivotar says. "But the next problem is how to get back out. We lost our lantern," he explains to Grum, "and we can't navigate these underground passages without light."

"Very nearby a place is where a torch we can get."

"Great! Lead us there."

Grum leads them among the statues, toward an opening at the far end of the cavern. Suddenly, Juranda cries out. "Biv, look!"

"What is it?" asks Bivotar.

Juranda points at two small stone figures, poised in the middle of an argument. "It's Max and Fred!"

Bivotar stares in horror. "Oh, those poor elves!"

"Remember them, I do," says Grum.

Go to page 110.

"Among first to arrive were they. They must have just found a jade figurine. Thought they were playing did I, but they were merely fighting over figurine. Wanted to play also, did I, but before I could, spotted me had they, and turned to stone as now you see them."

Bivotar and Juranda are silent for a moment, thinking about Max and Fred. Finally, they turn away, and follow Grum.

The opening at the far end of the cavern leads into a short hallway, which ends at a round room with a domed ceiling. Sitting in

Go to page 111.

the center of the room, atop a pedestal, is a
flaming ivory torch. Four doorways lead from
the room, each one labeled with a signpost.
The signpost for the doorway they just left is
labeled

The Cavern
of the
Rainbow Mosses

The other three signposts read:

The Crypt of Death

The Dungeon of Dry Bones

The Hall of Mirrors

Juranda takes the ivory torch. "Now that
we've got light again, we can go back the way
we came."

"Just a second," says Bivotar. "What if we
run into Grawl or Leblong again? Maybe we
should take one of these other doorways instead." Bivotar thinks for a moment. "Well,
this is Grum's territory. Grum, do you have

Go to page 112.

any idea which exit to take?"

"Nothing about it does Grum know. Never beyond this point has Grum ever been."

Return to the Cavern of the Rainbow Mosses? Go to page 113.

Head for the Crypt of Death? Go to page 115.

Go to the Dungeon of Dry Bones? Go to page 117.

Head for the Hall of Mirrors? Go to page 119.

"On second thought, why don't we go back along the same route?" says Bivotar. "At least we're familiar with it."

Bivotar, Juranda, and Grum return to the Cavern of the Rainbow Mosses, and begin winding their way through the maze of stone figures again. Before they have crossed the cavern, however, a cold wind sweeps around them, and the amulet begins to glow. A moment later, an incredibly old man appears. He is wrinkled and stooped, and is dressed in a robe of midnight blue. Atop his head is an almost comical-looking pointed cap decorated with stars. He seemes harmless enough.

Then the old man speaks, in a powerful and malevolent voice that belies his innocent appearance. "At last I have found the thieves who ransacked my workshop! I will have to teach you that no one trifles with Grawl." He produces a wand from his robe and points it at Bivotar and Juranda, who turn into beetles. Grawl proceeds to crush them under his heel.

THE END

Your score is 9 out of a possible 10 points. Well, you probably deserve another chance. Turn to page 112 and try again.

"Okay, let's go this way," says Juranda, entering the doorway labeled "The Crypt of Death."

"Uh, doesn't that sound a little dangerous?" asks Bivotar, hesitating.

"Don't be such a yellow-belly, Biv."

Bivotar grumbles, but follows Juranda and Grum through the doorway. They enter a low tunnel, which ends a short while later at the entrance to a stone crypt. The entrance to the crypt is open, beckoning them to enter. Surrounding the entrance are numerous skulls, perched on poles. The skulls almost seem to be grinning at them.

They enter the crypt warily. An inscription on the wall reads:

HERE LIE THE FINAL REMAINS OF THE FLATHEADS
RULERS OF THE GREAT UNDERGROUND EMPIRE

Twelve stone coffins line the walls of the crypt.

With a reverberating slam, the enormous stone door shuts behind them. Several

Go to page 116.

months, or years, later, a caretaker wanders through and adds their skulls to the collection outside the door.

THE END

Your score is 9 out of a possible 10 points. Well, you probably deserve another chance. Turn to page 112 and try again.

"How about this door?" asks Bivotar, walking toward the exit labeled "The Dungeon of Dry Bones."

"I don't think I like the sound of that signpost," says Juranda.

"Oh, come on, if it looks dangerous, we'll come back and try another direction."

Go to page 118.

Juranda looks skeptical, but follows Bivotar and Grum through the doorway. They enter a long passage with roughly hewn walls. After walking for about ten minutes, Bivotar spots a shaft of light crossing the tunnel.

"What do you think about this light, Juran?"

"Beats me. I can't tell where it's coming from."

"Oh, well. Let's go on. There's still no end to this tunnel in sight."

They walk forward, and as soon as they cross the beam of light, the floor beneath them opens up! They fall into a long, smooth, sloping shaft. Down and down they slide, for what seems like an eternity. Finally, they land with a painful thud on a damp floor strewn with straw and human bones. After a long period, their bones join the others in the dungeon.

THE END

Your score is 9 out of a possible 10 points. Well, you probably deserve another chance. Turn to page 112 and try again.

"Well, the Hall of Mirrors sounds the safest to me," Bivotar decides. "Let's go that way."

They enter the passageway labeled "The Hall of Mirrors." Toward the beginning, the passage is low and narrow. However, it soon becomes wider and wider, and finally ends at a large room.

Bivotar and Juranda gasp as they enter the room—it is the banquet hall of the Castle of Zork! A gigantic mirror fills the far end of the room, just as they remember.

"Juran, how did we get back to the castle?"

"Something looks wrong, Biv. Look, that tapestry there belongs on the right side of the hall, but here it's on the left. And those windows, those are on the wrong side of the room, also!"

"Then this isn't the banquet hall of the castle!"

"No, it's an exact replica of the hall, only backwards—a mirror image! And buried here, far underground!"

Bivotar approaches the mirror. "Then that image there, on the other side of the mirror, that's the real banquet hall. If only there was

Go to page 120.

a way to get there. . . ." He reaches out toward the mirror. As his fingers touch the surface, there comes a rumble from deep within the earth. The room shakes, and all three are thrown to the floor.

When the floor stops shaking, Bivotar stands and looks around. "Juranda, we did it! This is the real banquet hall! We're back in the castle!"

Juranda looks around also. "Biv! Where's Grum? And who . . . who is that?"

Where Grum had been before the earthquake, there now stands a handsome young man, dressed in princely robes. Only his eyes seem familiar, filled with warmth and compassion. "I am Logrumethar," he states. "The enchantment is broken!"

They hear a cry from across the hall as Syovar enters. "Juranda! Bivotar! I felt that rumble and I came to investigate. I have been so worried. . . ." Syovar suddenly notices the figure in the princely garb. He freezes in his tracks, speechless. Then, he runs to Logrumethar and embraces him. "My son, my son," he cries, tears streaming from his eyes. "I

Go to page 122.

thought I should never see you again!"

* * *

That evening, Syovar holds a mighty banquet to celebrate the return of Logrumethar. Noblemen and enchanters from every township in the kingdom are present. Syovar and his son sit at the head table, flanked by Bivotar and Juranda.

"I don't understand exactly what happened," says Bivotar, between mouthfuls. "How was the enchantment broken?"

Syovar smiles broadly. "There are some things that even a warlock of Grawl's might cannot foresee."

"My father was right to send you into the Cavern of Doom. He, and he alone, felt that you would succeed where so many brave adventurers and mighty warriors had failed."

"In fact," continues Syovar, "the enchantment began to break when you demonstrated that your feelings for Grum as a person were more important than your feelings about his appearance."

"But it wasn't until you touched the mirror," Logrumethar adds, "and trans-

Go to page 124.

ported us back here, that the last of the curse was destroyed. Only then were my memories and appearance restored, and 'Grum' put to rest forever."

"And now," says Syovar, standing, "it is my turn to test my abilities." An expectant hush falls over the banquet hall. Syovar begins casting a spell, a spell so powerful that the very air in the room seems to crackle with energy. A cloud of smoke forms in the center of the hall. The cloud begins spinning around, swirling madly like a tiny tornado. It grows larger . . . and larger . . . and then suddenly it is gone!

In its place, standing in the center of the huge hall, looking dazed and confused, are a hundred or more explorers, treasure hunters, and knights. With one fantastic effort, Syovar has returned all the stone figures to life, and transported them back to the castle.

Suddenly, Bivotar and Juranda are buried under a mass of elvish hugs.

"Max!" shouts Juranda.

"Fred!" Bivotar yells.

"Max and Fred went exploring new under-

Go to page 126.

ground realm," explains Max. "Many dangers."

"Fred found this jade figurine," says Fred, holding it up.

"Wait a minute! Max found figurine." Max tries to snatch the figurine away from Fred.

"Did not! Fred saw it first!"

Syovar roars with laughter. "Calm down, you two, you'll destroy the entire castle if you keep fighting." He touches the jade figurine, and immediately each elf is holding an identical figurine.

"Maybe Fred did find it first," admits Max.

"But Max was maybe first to pick it up," Fred points out.

Syovar turns to Bivotar and Juranda. "Unfortunately, the time has come for us to say goodbye once again. I am now thrice indebted to you, but this time you have done a deed I value even more than my own life, returning to me my beloved son. I can never repay you, but return again and I shall certainly try." He hugs both of them warmly. "And don't forget the ring," he says, handing Juranda the Ring of Zork.

The world goes dark for a moment, and

Go to page 127.

then Bill and June are sitting on the ledge atop Lookout Point. The sun is beginning to sink low in the western sky. June looks at Bill, and slips the ring into her pocket. No words are necessary to share their feelings as they mount their bicycles for the ride home, for they know that they will soon visit the magical Kingdom of Zork again.

THE END

Your score is 10 out of a possible 10 points. Congratulations! You would make a fine adventurer.

Bivotars and Jurandas everywhere, your adventures have just begun!

If you've been brave and clever and lucky enough to get this far in the book, you may be ready for ZORK computer games from Infocom.

You'll find more excitement behind the magic door to ZORK than you'll ever find in any arcade. Infocom makes three ZORK games in all, as well as thrilling mysteries like DEADLINE™ and The WITNESS,™ and science fiction games like STARCROSS,™ SUSPENDED,™ and PLANETFALL.™

You can get Infocom games at just about any computer store. We make them for all kinds of computers: Apple II, Atari, Commodore 64, CP/M 8″, DEC Rainbow, DEC RT-11, IBM Personal Computer, NEC APC, NEC PC-8000, Osborne, TI Professional, TRS-80 Model I, and TRS-80 Model III. Be sure to buy the specially marked Infocom game that's right for your computer. And happy adventuring!

The next dimension.